D0296971

Thomas
AND THE TIGER

by Christopher Awdry
illustrated by Ken Stott

DEAN

One day Thomas heard some children talking about a
new wildlife park which was opening soon.
"It's going to have lions and tigers and even a hippo."

"What's a hippo?" Thomas asked.

"You'll soon see," said his driver. "We may have to carry some of the animals to the park ourselves."

Soon the animals began to arrive. Some came by lorry, and some by rail. The engines worked very hard, pulling extra trains to carry them.

One morning Thomas's driver was extra happy.
"We're going to the harbour today to collect something
for the wildlife park," he told Thomas.

At the harbour they found a big crate containing a tiger
and her cubs. The tiger had come from a zoo abroad.
A crane lifted the crate onto the truck and Thomas set off.

At the station Thomas waited while the big crate was unloaded. He was quite sad to see the tiger go.

He had been proud to carry such a noble and beautiful animal.

"I wonder if I shall see it again," he thought.

Near the station there was an old engine shed. The men used it for storing things they did not use very often.

Later, when Thomas was passing the shed he thought he saw something moving inside it. It seemed to look stripy.

Later that day Percy also passed the old engine shed.
He thought he saw some eyes glinting in the dark.

"I can't understand it," he told Thomas. "It was as if someone or something was watching me."

The next day Thomas was at the station. He was listening
to his driver talking to the fireman.

"It says in the newspaper that a tiger has escaped from the wildlife park," said the driver. "I wonder where it is?" Thomas smiled. He knew.

"Look in the old engine shed as we pass," he told his driver. When they came close, Thomas slowed down.

His driver looked out of the cab. "Why, it's the tiger and her cubs," he said. "That was very smart of you to find them, Thomas."

Thomas's driver told the Fat Controller about the tiger at once.

"We'd better let her keeper know she's safe," said the
Fat Controller.

A lorry came from the wildlife park to collect the tiger and her cubs. The keeper was very pleased.

"Well done, Thomas, for finding our tiger," he said, and the Fat Controller agreed.
"You've been a Really Useful Engine," he said.

Thomas often sees the tiger and her cubs when he passes the park now. He feels very proud to have rescued her.

As a special "thank you", the keeper named one of the tiger cubs Thomas.

Thomas

AND THE BIRTHDAY PARTY

by Christopher Awdry

illustrated by Ken Stott

"It's your driver's birthday on Saturday," said Percy.
"What is a birthday?" asked Thomas.
"It is the day when you get a year older," said Toby.

Thomas asked the fireman about the driver's birthday.
"His wife has baked him a cake," the fireman said.
"I wish I could see it," said Thomas.

"Let's give the driver a party at the station," said Toby.
"Then we can all see the cake," said Percy.
The fireman went to ask the stationmaster.

The stationmaster agreed. The engines were very
happy, but just two days before the birthday party the
Fat Controller sent Thomas away.

Thomas was sent to the big station to help out in the yard.
He was very upset.

At the big station Thomas worked hard all day.
He was looking forward to going home that evening.

But the Fat Controller did not send Thomas home.
He was needed to shunt trucks again the next day.

Thomas had to spend the night in the engine shed at the big station.

He could not go to sleep that night. "The driver will miss his party," he thought sadly.

The next day the Fat Controller came. "Well done, Thomas," he said. "You have been working very hard. I am pleased with you."

"Thank you, Sir," said Thomas. "But, when can I go home?"
"Don't worry, Thomas. I know all about your secret," said
the Fat Controller. "We will get you home in time."

Saturday came and everyone began to get ready for the party.
The stationmaster put up a sign saying HAPPY BIRTHDAY.

The porters decorated the engine shed and their children
blew up the balloons. At five o'clock everything was ready.

But when Thomas came home that evening there was
no sign of a party.

The shed doors were closed and everywhere was silent.
"What has happened?" Thomas asked.

The driver was just getting down from the cab when he saw his wife at the shed door.

She was carrying a big box. She took it into the shed and put it on the table.

The driver's wife took the lid off the box.
Thomas whistled loudly! "The cake looks just like me," he said.

Everyone sang "Happy Birthday" round the cake.
"It looks too good to cut," said the driver, but he did.

The children climbed into the carriage for the party.

The driver said it was the nicest birthday he had ever had.

Thomas was happy too.

James
AND THE BALLOONS

by Christopher Awdry

illustrated by Ken Stott

There was to be a balloon race on the Island of Sodor.
All the engines were very excited.

"I love balloons," said Thomas, "especially at parties when they go pop."
Gordon chuckled.

"But these are not party balloons," said Gordon.
"They are hot-air balloons with baskets fixed to them.
They carry people up into the sky."

James was chosen to take the balloons to their starting point. He was very proud.

"I wish I could watch the balloon race," he said.
"So do I," said his driver. "But we can't stop. We have
work to do."

Later that afternoon, as James puffed down the line, he saw the balloons gently rising into the air.

"Can't we stop and watch for a while?" James sighed.
"I'm sorry, James," said his driver. "We're already late, we
 must move on."

The balloons were high in the sky now. They drifted overhead, but one sank very low.

"It looks as if that balloon is in trouble," said James.
His driver slowed down.

The balloon was almost down now. It bumped along the
ground and landed on the line right in front of James.
His driver put the brakes on.

"Thank you for stopping in time," shouted one of the balloonists. "It looks as if we are out of the race though."

"Never mind," replied James's driver. "We'll take you and your balloon to the finish."

James's driver and fireman helped the balloonists to pack their gear away.

Then they all heaved the heavy bundle onto the train.

The balloonists climbed into the guard's van and James started off again.

James reached the finish just in time to see the other balloons landing.

Lots of children were there to cheer the winner.

Thomas and the Fat Controller were there too.

"This is much more exciting than party balloons,"
said Thomas. The Fat Controller agreed.

"And even more exciting if you rescue a balloon and bring it home," said James.

The Fat Controller laughed. "Well done, James," he said.